RUSSELL AYTO PRESENTS
(in order of intelligence)

A clever mouse.

Some other animals.

Mr and Mrs Homeowner.

Mr Bosh, Big Chief Mouse-Catcher.

And Mr Bumble,

Assistant Mouse-Catcher

(wearing shoes that squeak like a mouse).

For the MOUSEHOLE WILD BIRD HOSPITAL
(Registered Charity 272145)

MOUSE IN THE HOUSE

RUSSELL AYTO

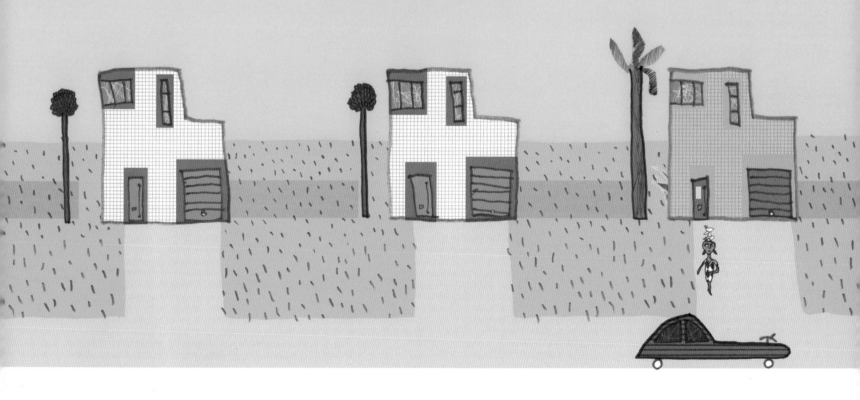

Andersen Press

A van pulls up outside the *wrong* house
and out **stumble** the two catchers of mice:

Mr Bosh

and Mr Bumble.

Mr Bosh reads the note stuck to the *right* door.

"Mouses shouldn't be in houses," says Mr Bumble.

"Well, you go in and set the traps...

and **SNAP!**

That will be *that*," says Mr Bosh.

But

the **mouse**

is too

clever

for

the

traps.

The traps

only catch

something that **treads**

on them.

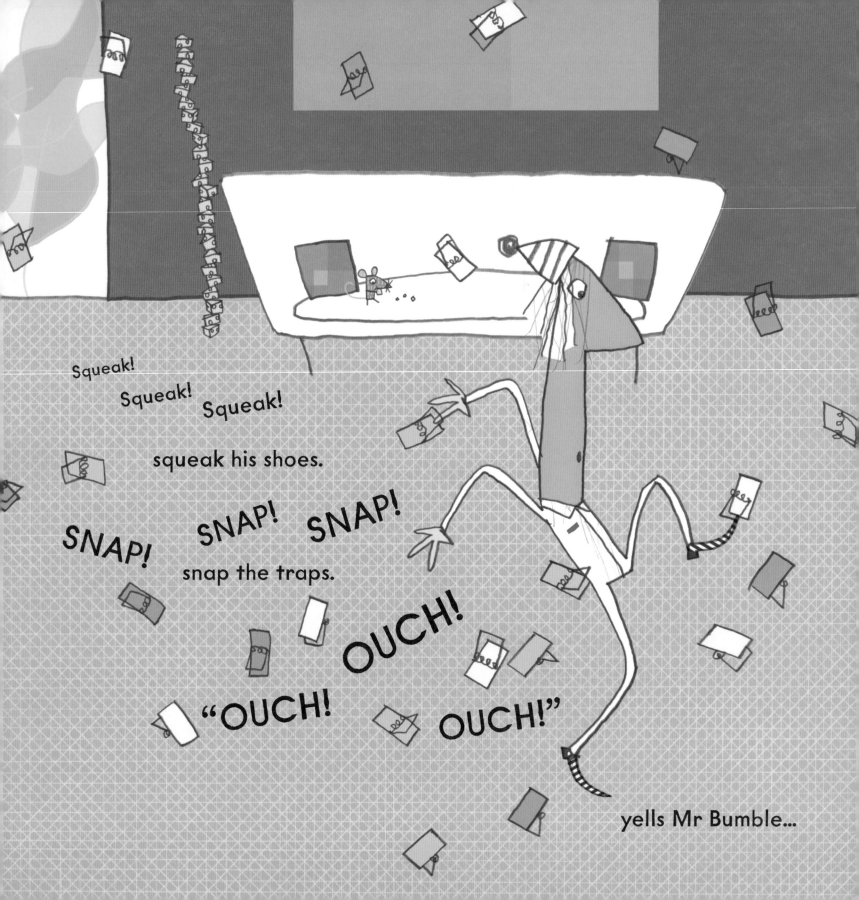

"I forgot about *dose* traps..."

"Never mind that," says Mr Bosh. "That mouse is clever. Go and get a cat instead. And that will be that."

"What's THAT?
That is NOT a cat."
says Mr Bosh.

"It's nearly a cat,"
says Mr Bumble.

"It's
a dog," says Mr Bosh.

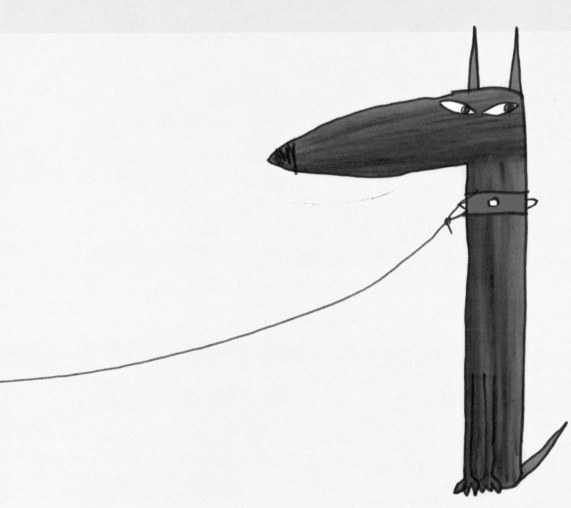

"Ah, but not *just* a dog," says Mr Bumble.

"It's a guard dog. 'Specially trained to protect houses from intruders."

"Okay," says Mr Bosh. "Put it in the house."

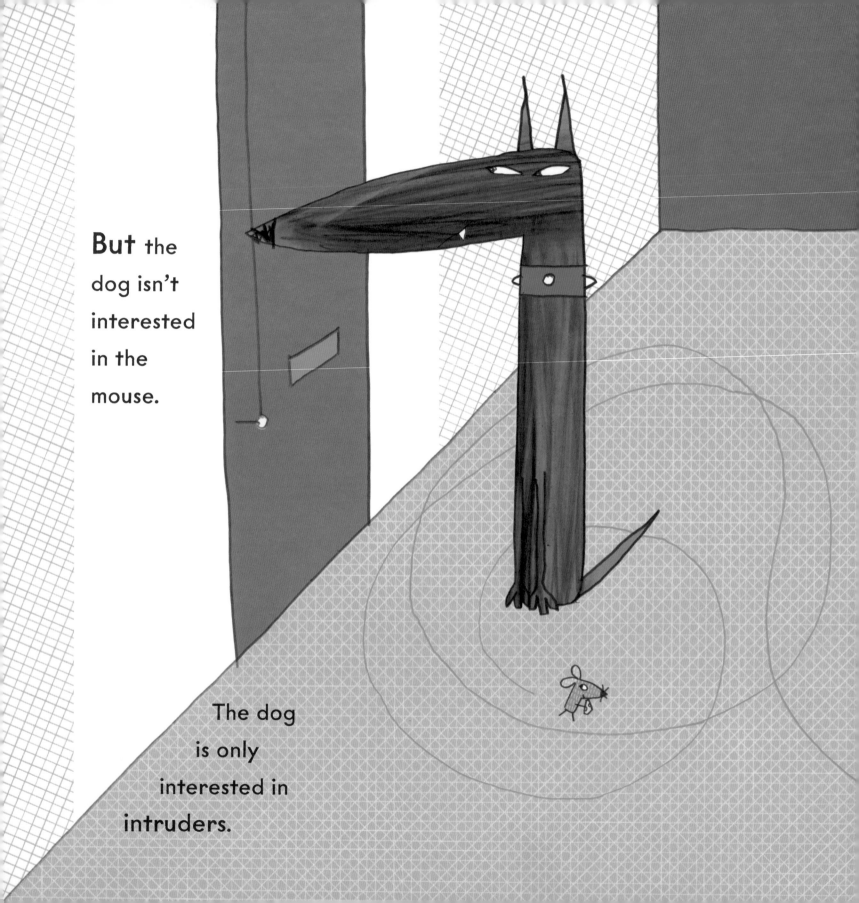

But the dog isn't interested in the mouse.

The dog is only interested in intruders.

"The dog is really well trained…"

"Never mind THAT," says Mr Bosh.

"I TOLD you to go and get a cat. And that will be **that.**"

"What's THAT?
That is NOT a cat."
says Mr Bosh.

"It is," says Mr Bumble. "It's a big cat."
"It's a tiger," says Mr Bosh.

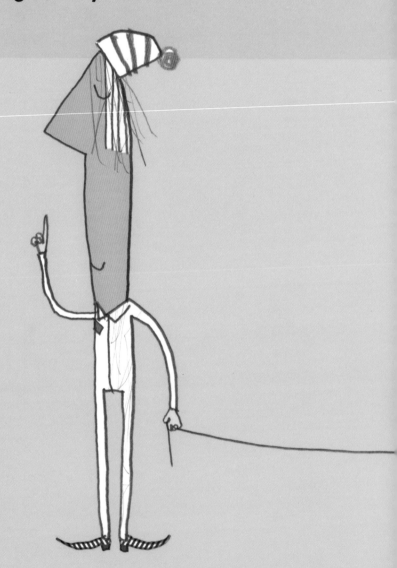

"Ah, but it's **still** a cat," says Mr Bumble. "And soon it will be hungry."

"Alright," Mr Bosh says. "Put it in the house."

But
the
tiger
isn't
interested

in

the

mouse.

The tiger is only interested
in bigger things to eat.

"The tiger did get hungry..."

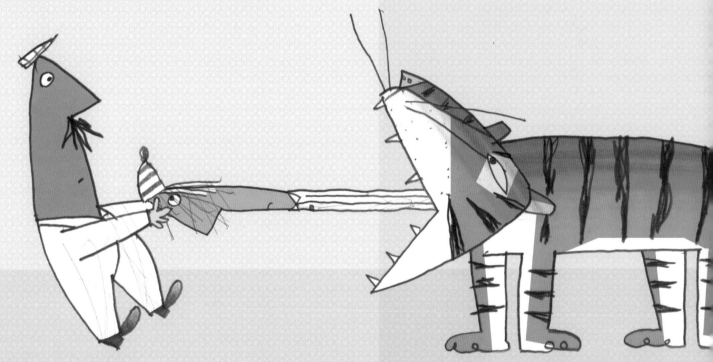

"Never mind
THAT!" says
Mr Bosh.
"Will you NOW go and get that CAT! And THAT will be THAT!"

"Now WHAT? THAT is most definitely NOT a cat!" says Mr Bosh.

"Well, it's the next best thing!" says Mr Bumble.

"It's an ELEPHANT!" says Mr Bosh. "And aren't elephants frightened of mice?"

"I don't know about that," says Mr Bumble. "But I do know it will **squash** the mouse **flat.** And that will be **that.**"

"RIGHT!" says Mr Bosh. "Put it in the house."

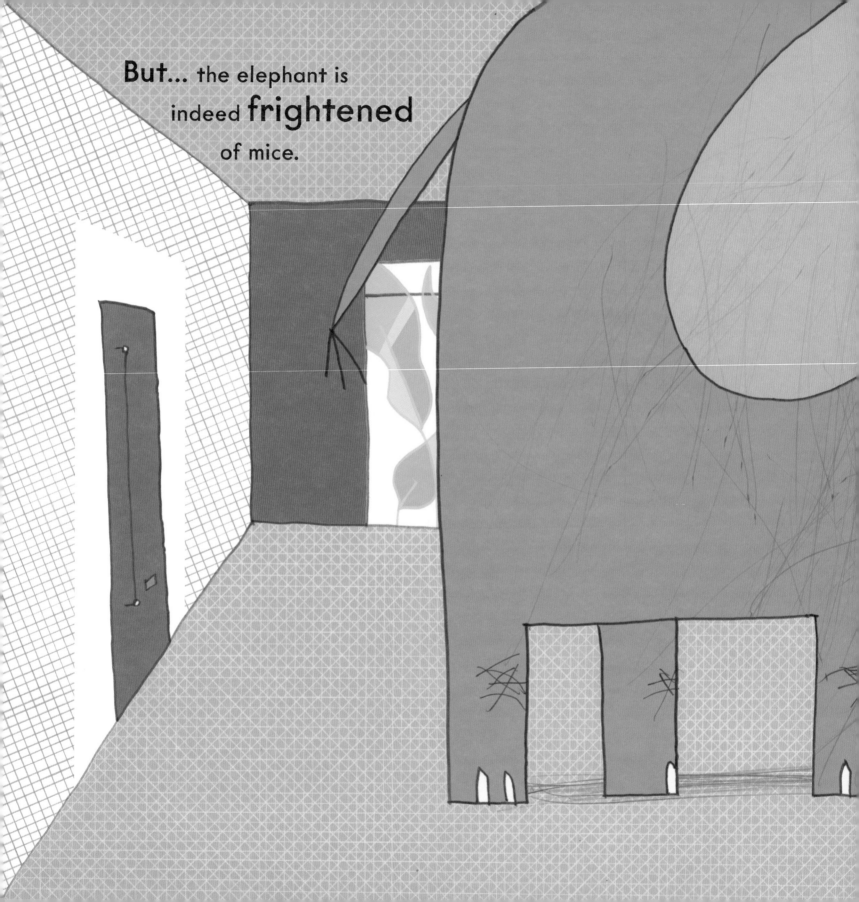

But... the elephant is indeed **frightened** of mice.

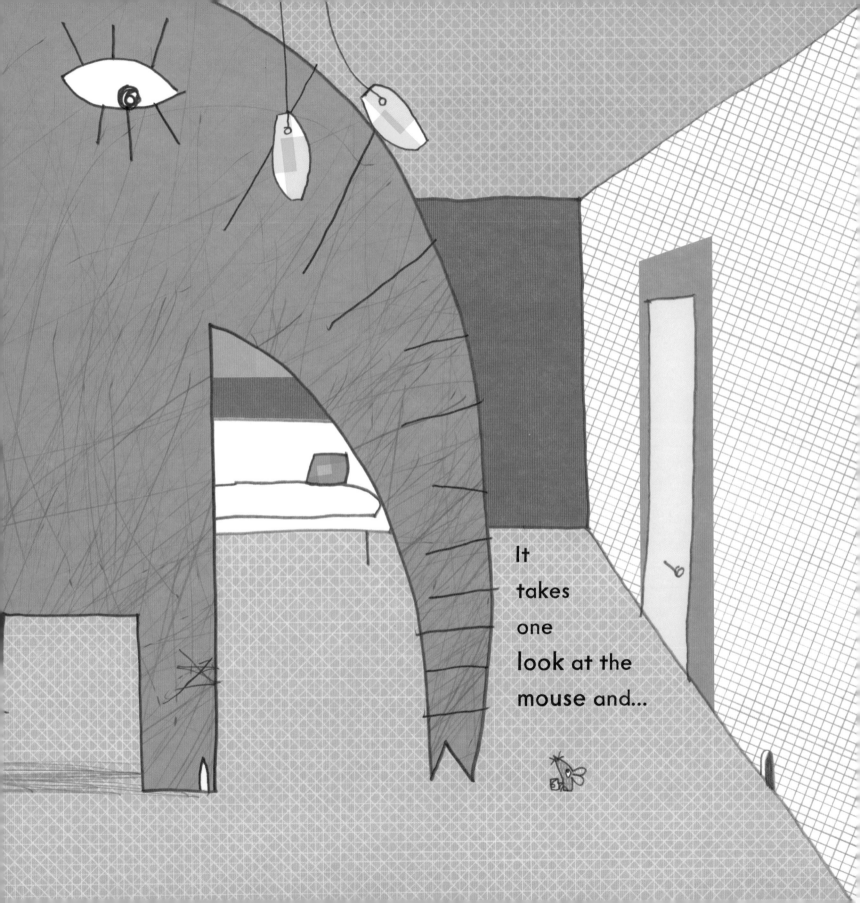

It
takes
one
look at the
mouse and...

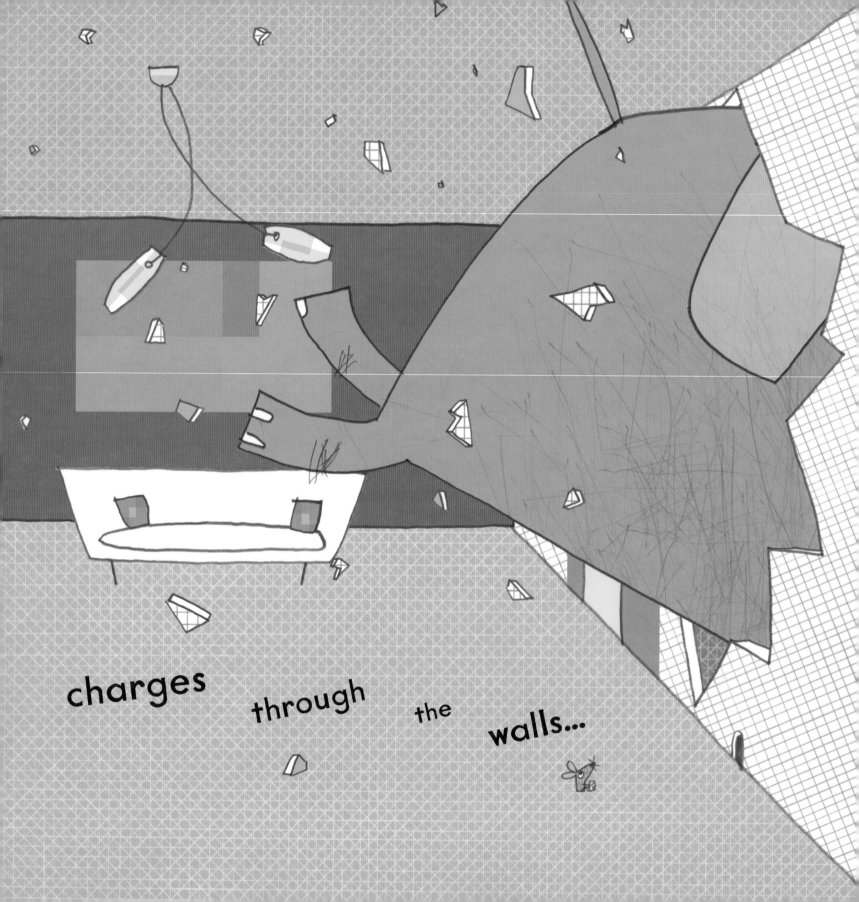

charges through the walls...

Bringing
the
whole
house
down...

FLAT.

And that...

in the end...

is that.

END
(no animals were harmed in the making of this book)